A Little Seed

Lucille Rayner

With Best Wishes
Lucille Rayner

1

A Little Seed

British Library Cataloguing in Publication Data.

A CIP catalogue record for this book is available from the British Library.

Copyright © Lucille Rayner 2015

Published by East Anglian Press

ISBN: 978-0-9934934-3-0

Acknowledgements
Many thanks to:

My daughter, Fay, for her support, time and patience, and the lovely illustrations.

Suzan Collins from the Get Writing workshops who also inspired me to write.

Ann Bowyer for reading through.

Members of the Waveney Author Group.

Richard and Gina at the Coconut Loft Art Gallery and Coffee Lounge for their support, coffee and cake.

Jo Wilde: Editing
Fay Hewitt: Book illustrations and cover

Dedication

My late partner, John Bonsall, who inspired me to follow my dreams.

To my lovely grandchildren: Jermaine, Travis, Chantelle, Ashton, Lily-Kate and Jordan who gave me ideas to write this book.

Contents

A Little Seed

Chapter One
A little seed

Once I was a little seed waiting to be sown. I waited and waited until a gardener came along. He took me to the greenhouse, very large and warm it was. "What is going to happen to me?" I asked myself.

The gardener left me on a table and went away a while. He came back with a big bag, some water and a tray. Opening up the bag which was filled with soil, he picked me up with other seeds who I now call my friends, and planted us in the tray. The gardener then watered us till we were very wet.

A Little Seed

Something is happening to me, no longer a seed am I, because I am sprouting out everywhere. The gardener seems quite surprised. He waters us always, but I seem to be growing fast. I am bigger than my little friends who look at me and gasp. Here comes the gardener to water us again, he says I am a beauty and Matilda is my name.

Growing, growing, and growing! Getting bigger every day, now there is no more room for me to grow in this tray. The gardener realises that I am getting far too big; he takes me from the tray and plants me in a pot with a twig.

How nice, I can feel my roots spreading out. I will grow much bigger, of that I have no doubt. I wonder how big, and what I shall grow to be?

Can you guess?

As the days pass and the sun comes out, I can smell the scent of flowers and fruits growing in the greenhouse. Growing much, much bigger and faster by the day, I am taken from my little pot and put in a larger one today. "Matilda, my beauty you are growing very fast. Soon I shall be able to plant you in the ground, your home, at last," said the gardener.

I wonder where my home shall be and what am I? Weeks go by until the gardener says, "It's time, Matilda my beauty, to plant you in the ground and say goodbye." He puts me on a lorry with some friends that have grown like me and drives us to a little place by the beach and sea.

We are taken past a railway station to a road called Katwijk Way, a very busy roadside especially during the day. The gardener takes us from the lorry and lines us up like soldiers, looks at us with fondness, then plants us right away.

As I watch the gardener drive away, and leave me in my home, I know that I will be with friends and never be alone. My branches grow bigger and my roots too! Little leaves spring out, everywhere in view.

The gardener was right you know, a beauty I have turned out to be, along with all my other friends on the roadside just like me. I look at myself and to my surprise am happy as can be, I know, have you guessed it?

YES!

A TREE THAT'S ME!

A Little Seed

Chapter Two
What a perfect day

Matilda looked about her and sighed. This is my home now what can I see? Looking in front of me I see a library with lots of books to read, people coming and going, arms full, what can they be reading I wonder?

Could it be stories to read to the children, history, geography, cooking or joke books, to name but a few? A place to be quiet, a place to read a magazine or a comic, use the computer or go to the café for a snack and a drink.

There is a large car park in front of me which is filling up with cars of all shapes and sizes and colours too!

Motorbikes in the corner standing proud, people getting parking tickets for the time they are allowed.

Here comes the parking attendant to look at the cars, he checks tickets for time and date and gives you a bigger ticket if you are late.

A Little Seed

On the road, a bus full of passengers and packages too, I wonder where they are going? Could it be the zoo? Maybe they have been shopping, going to work or school or off to see a friend. The houses behind me, people go in and out, walking into town or just down the road. Bleep, bleep, bleep! goes the pelican crossing. I watch a lady cross with a pushchair and a child in tow, also a man walking his bike. HEY! Wait a minute, you don't walk a bike. I am sure you sit on it and ride it, what a funny man!

A Little Seed

Looking up and down the road I see the traffic in a large queue, buses, lorries, cars and bikes all waiting to move so as not to be late. Train standing at the station waiting for passengers to board, seagulls flying overhead making a noise. Offices, there are many, I wonder what goes on there? I can see through the window: ladies and gentlemen sitting in chairs.

A Little Seed

Learner drivers are arriving to take their tests looking very nervous, but I am sure they will do their best.

In the distance I see a church spire standing very tall, and a wind turbine turning to power us all.

This is what I can see in my home today, the sun is shining in a bright blue sky, all my friends are happy and so am I.

Ahh! WHAT A PERFECT DAY!

A Little Seed

Chapter Three
Home to many

Now, I have settled in my home and am fully grown. I have made so many friends, some of whom live on me in holes, leaves and branches.

There are ants who make their home under my roots. They are very busy making a nest and sometimes tickle me and never seem to rest.

Birds flying high land on me before flying on or make a nest for their young, they sing and play and make my day.

A Little Seed

Seagulls flying high, making loud noises and looking for food. They poo everywhere, on me, the floor, cars, buildings and even people, they don't say "Please may I poo?" they just do it and make a nasty mess and NEVER go to the loo.

A Little Seed

One night Mr Fox came by to say "Hello."

He roams the streets at night you know, he has a beautiful bushy tail and shiny eyes, if you see him you will be very surprised. He doesn't like people and sometimes hides in the trees for he is a wild animal, but always a good friend to me.

A Little Seed

Here comes Spencer the spider to spin his web on me. He will try to catch flies and bugs and have them for his tea.

"Hello Matilda how are you today?"

"Very well thank you Spencer, it's such a lovely day."

The car park full as the market is open, people coming and going arms full of shopping, children in tow. Traffic up and down the road is very busy, sometimes a traffic jam and women walking past me pushing their prams.

Ahh! much to see, I love being a tree. My leaves are rustling in a cool breeze, they look beautiful to me. Two leaves that hang on me I call Burt and Ernie, they hang on my longest branch which stretches out into the road, and sometimes need to hang on tight as buses and lorries go by.

"HANG ON!" Ernie said to Burt, "It's a big lorry and he is a bit close. We must breathe in or we will get knocked off our branch or come loose."

"Whew!" Burt replied, still hanging on.

A Little Seed

There are lots of creatures living on me, some you may know and some you cannot see. There are beetles, caterpillars and spiders of all kinds, woodlice, birds and even mice sometimes.

The worms William and Wendy and their family make tunnels under my roots and are friends with their neighbours the ants. They wriggle and tickle but get in a pickle when the birds come to eat.

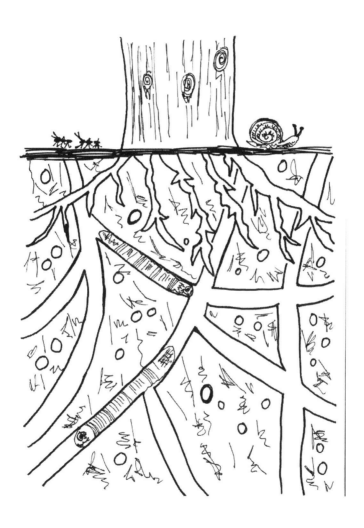

The seagulls are noisy again and always want to eat, they do a stamping dance with their feet. This brings the worms to the surface for the seagulls and other birds to feast. What a treat! How can I be lonely here on the street, for there is never a dull moment. I am home to many and friend to lots more. My life as a tree is never a bore.

A Little Seed

Chapter Four
Autumn to winter

Cloudy and grey: I guess rain is on its way. Summer has gone, all the holiday makers too. Most people have coats on and umbrellas with them today. The last of the birds fly high and coo.

Leaves are falling and changing colour, green to yellow, orange and brown, most rustling and blowing in the breeze then slowly falling to the ground. Leaves on the roadside, they are swirling round and round. How beautiful they look, the colours very bright and grand.

A Little Seed

Autumn is upon us and the nights get darker too, I can hear those noisy seagulls and they are not asking for the loo! Soon my branches will be bare and winter will appear. Wind, rain, sleet and snow all come at this time of year.

A Little Seed

I rest a while until the spring when my buds then re-appear. They grow into beautiful leaves then start the cycle for another year.

If you are ever in the town or passing in a car or bus, give me a wave and a smile. Just take a look around to see all that my friends and I can see. Remember not so long ago, I was just a little seed.

A Little Seed

Dear Reader,

If you have enjoyed reading this book, then tell all your friends, tweet about it, and please leave a review on Amazon.

Thank you.

About The Author

Lucille is a Support Worker and assists and supports older people. She loves holidays in the sunshine, family get-togethers and walking in the Suffolk countryside.

Lucille enjoys writing in her spare time and recently wrote a chapter for a children's book entitled 'Little Kitty the Cat Burglar' with all royalties going to Alzheimer's research UK. ISBN: 978-0993169076

Lucille is currently writing a story for a mystery book for charity and also another children's book.
To find out more about Lucille, or to follow her on social media, visit her author:
https://www.facebook.com/Lucille-Rayner-362171100645432/timeline/

Printed in Great Britain
by Amazon.co.uk, Ltd.,
Marston Gate.